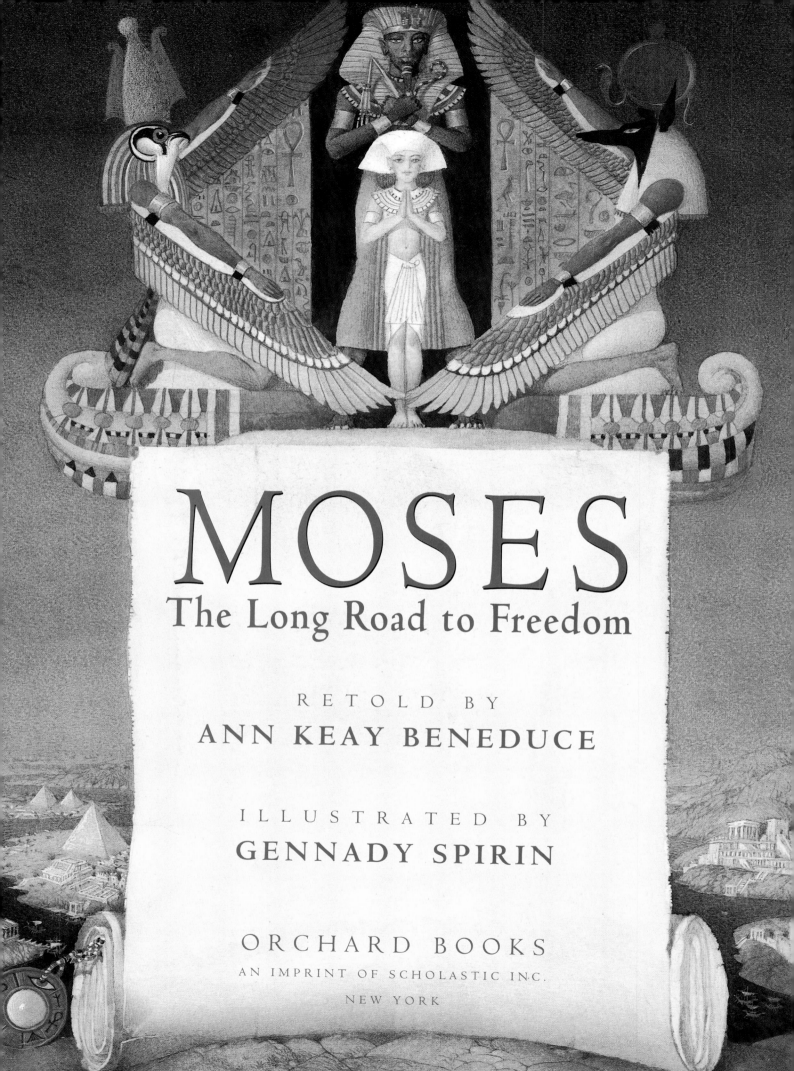

MOSES
The Long Road to Freedom

RETOLD BY
ANN KEAY BENEDUCE

ILLUSTRATED BY
GENNADY SPIRIN

ORCHARD BOOKS
AN IMPRINT OF SCHOLASTIC INC.
NEW YORK

For joel,

who has helped so many

to find freedom. . . .

A. K. B.

To my son, Gennady,

who graduated from

Princeton High School.

G. S.

The young mother kissed her sleeping baby tenderly, and then placed him in a wicker basket, which she set carefully into the water at the edge of the Nile River.

"Farewell, my beautiful son," she whispered. "Now you will be safe. You were not born to become a slave."

Then she hid and watched as the basket, with its precious passenger, was carried gently down the stream. Soon, just as she had hoped, it came to rest not far away. It was caught behind some reeds near the riverbank.

Now it happened that on that same afternoon, the royal princess — daughter of the Pharaoh, the ruler of ancient Egypt — was about to go swimming in the Nile with some of her friends when she saw a basket floating in the water.

"Oh, look!" cried the princess. "There's a baby in that basket! It must be the child of one of our Hebrew slaves! But we can't let him drown. I'll take him home and bring him up myself. I'll name him Moses, meaning 'drawn from the water'."

"You will need a nurse to care for him," said a little girl who was standing nearby. "I know just the person to help you. Shall I go and get her?"

"Yes, please," said the princess. "I will pay her well to nurse this special baby." The clever little girl was, in fact, the baby's older sister, Miriam. And the woman that the princess hired to nurse little Moses was his real mother.

Moses quickly became a favorite of the Pharaoh, who treated him like one of his own family. This meant that he received a fine education and was trained to be a leader.

But, while Moses was treated like an Egyptian prince, he knew that he was really the child of a Hebrew slave. And he also knew that most of the Hebrew people were being forced to work very hard as slaves of the Egyptians.

One day, while he was still a young man, Moses got into a fight with one of the Pharaoh's guards, whom he saw beating a Hebrew worker very cruelly. Moses struck down the guard and rescued the worker, but the Pharaoh was displeased. Moses had to flee for his life. He went to the neighboring country of Midian, where he became a shepherd. He married and raised two sons, leading a peaceful and contented life in Midian for many years.

Back in Egypt, however, his people were still slaves. They longed to be free. The old Pharaoh whom Moses had known had died, and a new Pharaoh now ruled the country. The new Pharaoh was a proud, harsh ruler.

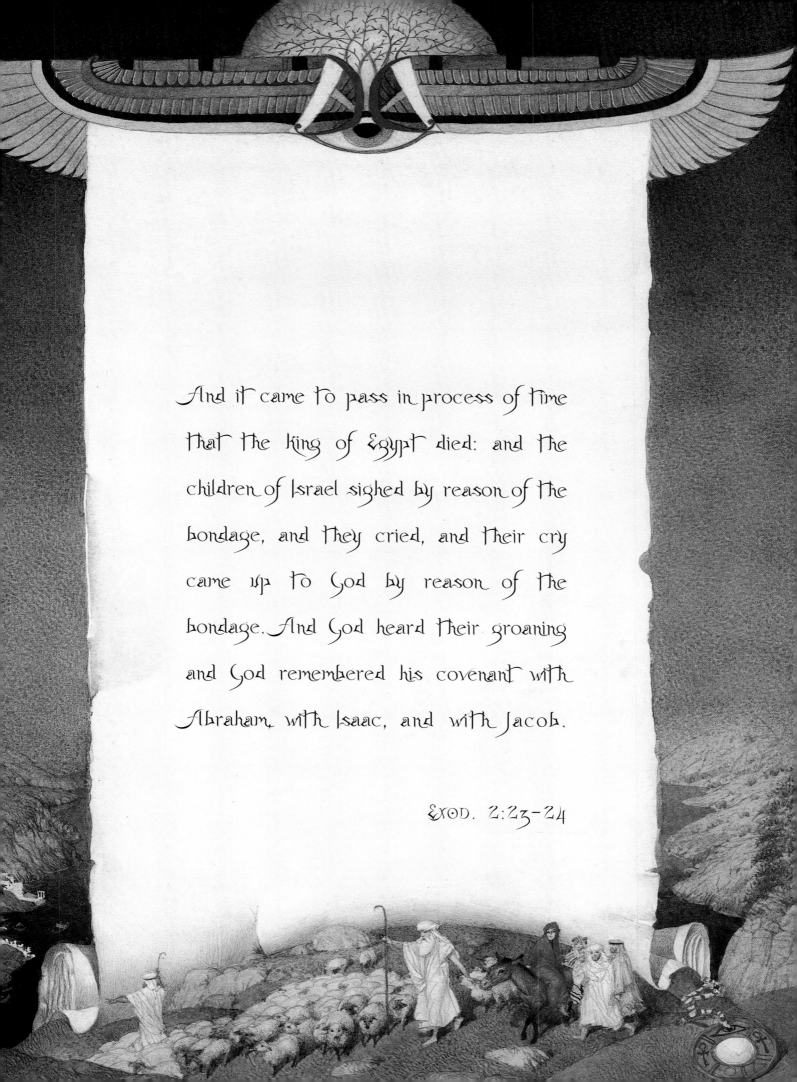

And it came to pass in process of time that the king of Egypt died: and the children of Israel sighed by reason of the bondage, and they cried, and their cry came up to God by reason of the bondage. And God heard their groaning and God remembered his covenant with Abraham, with Isaac, and with Jacob.

Exod. 2:23-24

One day, Moses was minding his sheep as they grazed on the slopes of Mount Sinai when he saw a bush that seemed to be on fire. The bush was ablaze with light, yet, strangely, it was not at all harmed by the flames. As Moses walked toward it, he heard a voice. It was the voice of an angel of God. "Come no closer, Moses!" it ordered him. "And take off your sandals — you are standing on holy ground!"

Then God spoke to Moses. "Your people are still suffering in Egypt, while you enjoy a pleasant life in Midian," He said. "You must go back to Egypt and persuade the new Pharaoh to give the Hebrew slaves their freedom."

"But this is a very difficult task!" protested Moses. "I am getting old, and I am not a good speaker. Why have You chosen me to do it?"

"I have chosen you for good reasons. Take your brother, Aaron, with you. He is a very fluent speaker — he can speak for you if need be."

"But this new Pharaoh is a proud and stubborn ruler. Even if I tell him that You have sent me, he will not readily agree to do what I ask," said Moses. "I will need to do something to show him Your marvelous power — something to make him respectful."

"Here is a marvel that you can perform yourself, Moses. I see you have your rod with you. Throw it on the ground!"

Moses did so and, to his surprise, the rod became a huge, hissing snake.

"Now pick it up!" Moses gingerly picked up the snake by its tail, and the fearsome creature became just a rod in his hand once more.

Moses was satisfied. He agreed to do what God had asked. And soon he, his wife, and sons set out for Egypt, where they were met by Moses's brother, Aaron. Moses was welcomed back by his people, who were overjoyed to hear his plan to lead them to freedom. He and Aaron soon arranged a meeting with the new ruler of Egypt.

"Why have you come here?" demanded the Pharaoh.

"Our God has sent us to ask you to free your Hebrew slaves," said Aaron. "They have worked for you for many years, but now they wish to go to another land, where they can worship their own God and live in peace."

"I am more powerful than any God of yours. Why should I obey Him? What can He do that I cannot do myself?" asked the Pharaoh.

Moses was expecting this question. In reply, he turned his rod into a terrifying snake, and then back again into a rod. But this wondrous feat did not impress the Pharaoh. In fact, it only made him more stubborn and he declared that he would never free his slaves. Instead, to punish them for even having asked for freedom, he made the poor Hebrews work harder than ever. Of course, they were disappointed and angry with Moses.

Moses and Aaron were disappointed, too. They went back to the Pharaoh. This time it was Aaron who turned his rod into an enormous snake to show God's power, but still the Pharaoh was not impressed.

"My own magicians can do this easy trick," he declared, and he ordered them to do so. But the snakes that the magicians produced were small, and Aaron's huge snake ate them all.

Even then, however, the Pharaoh did not change his mind. "I will never let the Hebrew slaves go!" he declared. "I don't have to obey your God."

Now God was very angry. He said to Moses, "I'll show this stubborn ruler what happens to those who don't obey God! Tell Aaron to take his rod and, while the Pharaoh is watching, hold it out over the Nile." When Moses and Aaron did as God told them, the water in the river instantly turned to blood. The fish that were in the river died, a foul smell arose, and the Egyptians could no longer drink from the river. And all over the country, in the streams, in the ponds, in the wells, and in every pool of water, every pail and pot, the water also turned to blood. Soon the thirsty Egyptians became ill. Only Goshen, the section of the country where the Hebrews lived, was spared; the slaves had all the pure water they needed.

After a week, Moses took pity on the Egyptians' suffering, and he asked God to end their punishment. Then he went again to the Pharaoh.

"You see what God can do if He is not obeyed. Now, won't you agree to let my people go?" he asked. But the proud Pharaoh still refused.

So, once again, God showed the Pharaoh His anger, and Egypt was stricken with a new punishment. This time, God sent an invasion of frogs. Out of the rivers and ponds they came in unbelievable numbers, hopping into people's houses and beds, into their ovens, into their pots, and even into the bread dough the servants were kneading. The fields and roads were covered, too, with the slippery, slimy creatures. It was impossible to walk, as frogs crowded under and into every boot and shoe. But the Pharaoh was still not willing to let his slaves go.

So God sent more punishments. First, the Egyptians were infested with lice. Then they were bitten by fleas and harassed by swarms of tiny flying insects: flies, midges, mosquitoes, and gnats. Next, all their cattle became sick. Then painful boils broke out on people's bodies. The Pharaoh's magicians and priests had to admit that they could not stop these new misfortunes — in fact, they themselves were ill. Finally the Pharaoh agreed that, if only God would stop these terrible afflictions, the slaves could have their freedom and leave the country.

"But they must leave their flocks of sheep and cattle here, in payment for their freedom," he declared. Of course, Moses could not agree to this.

"That is not fair," Moses replied. "In return for all our years of hard work, you must not only let us take our flocks and other possessions with us, but you should also supply us with all that we will need for the journey."

At this, the Pharaoh grew angry. He refused once more to let his slaves go. So God decided to punish him again. This time he told Moses to point his rod toward the sky. As soon as Moses did so, God sent a storm over all of Egypt, except for the places where the Hebrews lived. It was the worst storm anyone had ever seen. As thunder crashed and rumbled, bolts of lightning set fields, barns, and houses on fire. Rain and hail poured down, breaking branches from the trees, striking down cattle, horses, and people, and even killing the grass and crops in the fields. It went on for days, and then weeks, without a sign of stopping.

The Pharaoh called Moses and Aaron to his palace and pleaded with them to ask God to stop the storm. "It was wrong of me to disobey your God," confessed the Pharaoh. "You are right — I have been wicked. Please go and beg God to end this terrible storm, and I will let you and your people go to freedom."

Moses said, "You have seen God's awesome power. I will ask God to stop the thunder and the lightning and the hail. I will do this because I feel sorry for your people. But as for you, I still find it hard to believe that you will really keep your promise and let my people go."

And, just as Moses suspected, as soon as the storm ended, the Pharaoh changed his mind. So God called up a great wind from the east that carried swarms of hungry locusts into the fields to devour what was left of the Egyptians' crops. Never had anyone seen so many locusts. Soon there was not a green herb or blade of grass to be found in the fields, nor even a single leaf left on any tree. Now the Pharaoh saw that his people were truly in danger of starving. He begged Moses to rid the country of the locusts, and in return, of course, he promised to let the Hebrews go. Moses took pity on the Egyptians again, and asked God to forgive the Pharaoh. Immediately, God sent a strong west wind that blew all the locusts away and into the Red Sea. There wasn't a locust left anywhere in Egypt. But, as soon as the locusts were gone, the Pharaoh once again regretted his promise and refused to let the slaves go.

Then God said to Moses, "Stretch up your hand to the heavens, and I will bring down on this earth a darkness so thick it can be felt." So Moses stretched his hand toward the sky — and at once the sun disappeared and a deep darkness fell over the land and the sea.

It was so dark that the Egyptians did not dare to come out of their homes. They could see nothing at all. They tried to light their lamps, but without success — every fire and flame had gone out. But all the Hebrews still had light in their houses.

After three days, God ended the darkness. Then the Pharaoh called Moses to his palace and said, "Go and tell the Hebrew workers that soon they will no longer be my slaves, but free men. They can take their entire families — only their flocks of sheep and their cattle must be left behind."

"But what kind of freedom is this that you offer? You know that we cannot leave without our flocks and our cattle — we would starve to death!" exclaimed Moses. "I have told you before that we need them, as we will have no other way to make our living or to make offerings to God!"

But when the Pharaoh heard this, he withdrew his offer once again. So the Hebrew slaves were still not free.

Now, finally, God's patience was at an end. He decided to send a terrible punishment: a plague that would destroy every firstborn animal and child belonging to the Egyptians. But first He warned Moses.

"Tell the Hebrews to smear the blood of a lamb on the lintels over the doors of their houses," God ordered. "When I see this, it will be a sign to me. My angels and I will pass over those houses and the plague will not hurt anyone inside them. But at midnight I shall smite the Egyptians. Even the Pharaoh's eldest son will die."

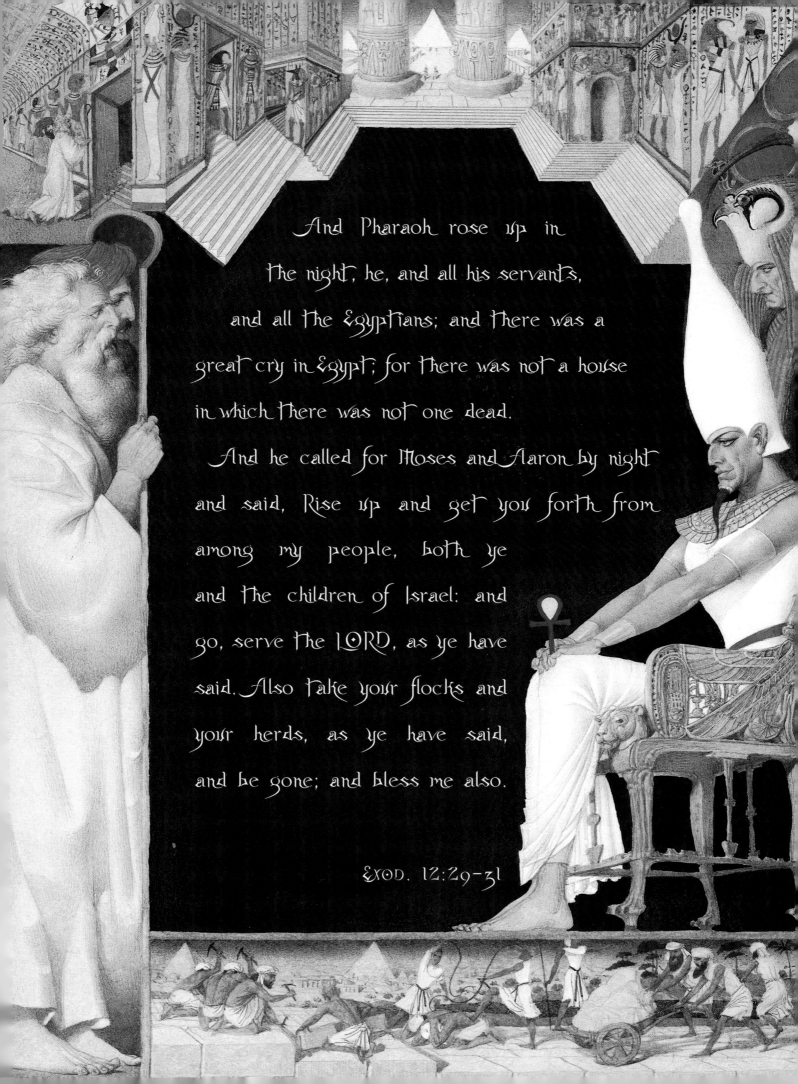

And Pharaoh rose up in
the night, he, and all his servants,
and all the Egyptians; and there was a
great cry in Egypt; for there was not a house
in which there was not one dead.

And he called for Moses and Aaron by night
and said, Rise up and get you forth from
among my people, both ye
and the children of Israel: and
go, serve the LORD, as ye have
said. Also take your flocks and
your herds, as ye have said,
and be gone; and bless me also.

EXOD. 12:29-31

The next morning, there was no Egyptian household that had not suffered at least one death. The Pharaoh, grieving over his own dead son, agreed at last to let the Hebrew slaves go. This time he seemed to be sincere.

So the Hebrews and their families, headed by Moses and Aaron, set out at last on the road to freedom. God led them each day, wrapped in a pillar of cloud, and at night He lit their way with a pillar of fire. They were a large group, approximately six hundred thousand strong. They went across the Egyptian border to Succoth, and from there to Etham and Baal-Zephon. But even there they did not feel entirely safe, so they continued on their way. Finally they arrived at the edge of the Red Sea. On the other side of the deep sea lay freedom.

But in the meantime, the Pharaoh and his advisers decided they had made a great mistake in letting their slaves leave. Suddenly they realized how valuable the Hebrews' work had been.

"Stop them! Don't let those slaves get away!" the Pharaoh commanded. His army set off on horseback, galloping after the departing Hebrews. Soon they had nearly caught up with the Hebrews, who were traveling on foot and so were much slower.

To their alarm, the Hebrews now saw that they were trapped between the enemy behind them and the deep sea ahead of them.

"Have you brought us all this way only to have us killed?" they cried to Moses. But Moses had faith that God would save them.

"Lift up your rod and stretch out your hand over the sea, and the waters will be divided," God told him. "You and your people will be able to walk on dry ground right through the middle of the sea."

And as soon as Moses raised his rod, a great wind blew out of the east. The wind divided the waters of the Red Sea, leaving a path of dry earth in between the high walls of water on either side. All the Hebrews ran across the path to safety, with their cattle and flocks of sheep behind them.

When they reached the other shore, the people turned around and looked back to see how closely the Pharaoh's army was following them. To their astonishment, they saw the horses and soldiers floundering in the waves as the walls of water closed on them. Every Egyptian soldier was drowned. But all the Hebrews had been spared.

Moses's sister, Miriam, and some of the other women took up their tambourines and began to dance for joy. Thousands of Hebrew voices joined and rose in a prayer of thanks to God for saving them. It became a song called "The Song at the Sea."

"Sing ye to God, for He hath triumphed gloriously!" it began.

The Hebrew people were free at last. Slaves no more, they were free to go and live on their own land, and to worship God in their own way.

EPILOGUE

The biblical story of Moses and his people does not end here. With God's help, Moses had rescued the Hebrews from their slavery in Egypt, but this intelligent and charismatic leader knew that his duties were not yet finished. Next he must find a homeland for them.

Much earlier, before their ancestors had left their homes in Canaan and gone to Egypt, God had promised the Hebrews that He would give them Canaan as their permanent homeland. Now, with God's help and the leadership of Moses and his brother, Aaron, the former slaves set out for the long journey back to their Promised Land.

Approximately three months after leaving Egypt, they arrived at Mount Sinai, where God revealed to Moses the Ten Commandments. God also asked that the people build Him a dwelling place — a tabernacle — so that He could live among them. They did this, and then they continued their journey, which took nearly forty years.

Finally they reached Moab, on the shore of the Jordan River.

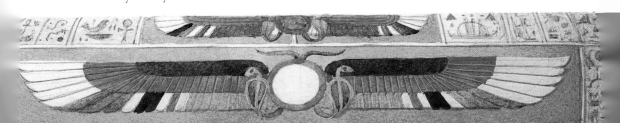

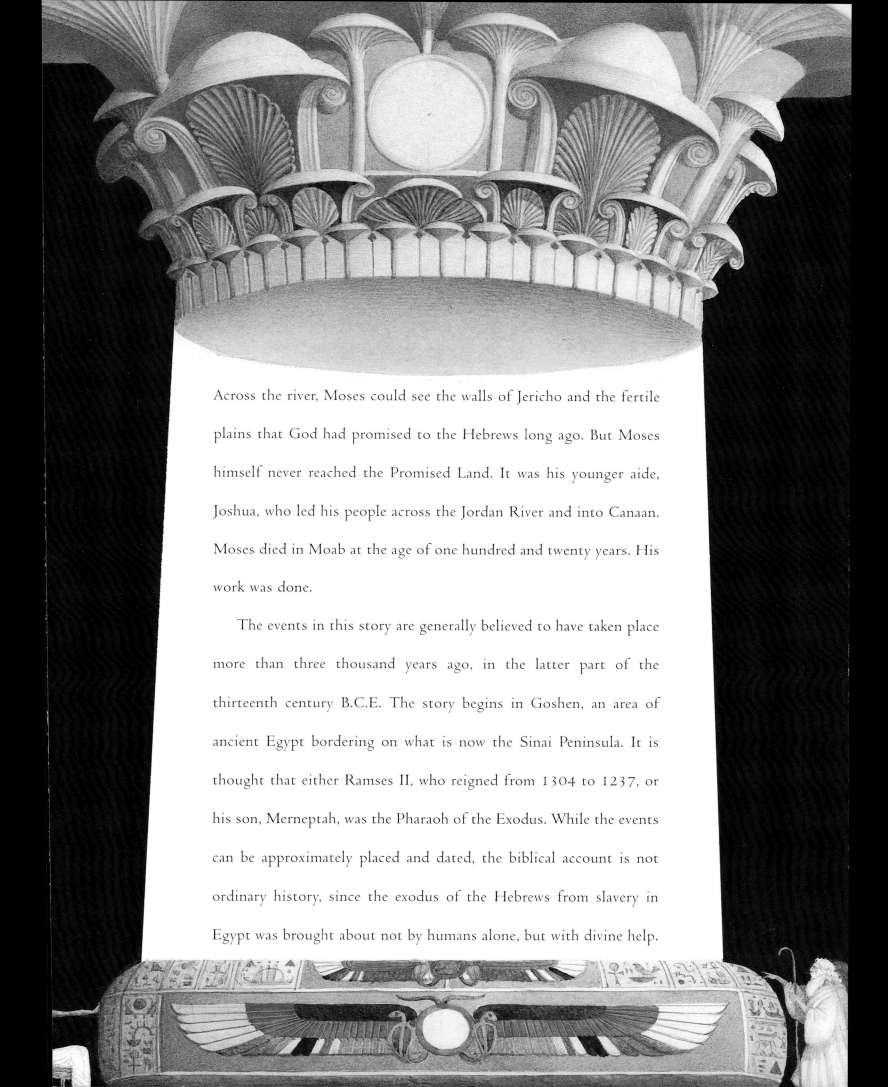

Across the river, Moses could see the walls of Jericho and the fertile plains that God had promised to the Hebrews long ago. But Moses himself never reached the Promised Land. It was his younger aide, Joshua, who led his people across the Jordan River and into Canaan. Moses died in Moab at the age of one hundred and twenty years. His work was done.

The events in this story are generally believed to have taken place more than three thousand years ago, in the latter part of the thirteenth century B.C.E. The story begins in Goshen, an area of ancient Egypt bordering on what is now the Sinai Peninsula. It is thought that either Ramses II, who reigned from 1304 to 1237, or his son, Merneptah, was the Pharaoh of the Exodus. While the events can be approximately placed and dated, the biblical account is not ordinary history, since the exodus of the Hebrews from slavery in Egypt was brought about not by humans alone, but with divine help.

ABOUT THE RETELLING

The two main sources of reference used in this retelling are *The Torah, Modern Commentary* (edited by W. Gunther Plaut, Union of American Hebrew Congregations, New York, 1981) and *The Holy Bible, King James Version* (Viking Studio/Caxton Pennyroyal Press, New York, 1999). While the story of the Exodus has been retold here in fictionalized form and with contemporary language, it is strongly hoped and intended that readers will be inspired to return to one of the great traditional versions to read the full, rich account of this and many other events in the life of Moses.

All rights reserved. Published by Orchard Books, an imprint of Scholastic Inc. ORCHARD BOOKS and design are registered trademarks of Watts Publishing Group, Ltd., used under license. SCHOLASTIC and associated logos are trademarks and/or registered trademarks of Scholastic Inc. No part of this publication may be reproduced, or stored in a retrieval system, or transmitted in any form or by any means, electronic, mechanical, photocopying, recording, or otherwise, without written permission of the publisher. For information regarding permission, write to Orchard Books, Scholastic Inc., Permissions Department, 557 Broadway, New York, NY 10012.
LIBRARY OF CONGRESS CATALOGING-IN-PUBLICATION DATA AVAILABLE
0-439-35225-8

10 9 8 7 6 5 4 3 2 1   04 05 06 07 08
Printed in Singapore   46
Reinforced binding for library use
First Scholastic edition, February 2004

The illustrations were created in pencil and watercolor on a French paper called Arches. The text type is set in 13-point Venetian301 BT and Swashbuckler. Book design by Marijka Kostiw